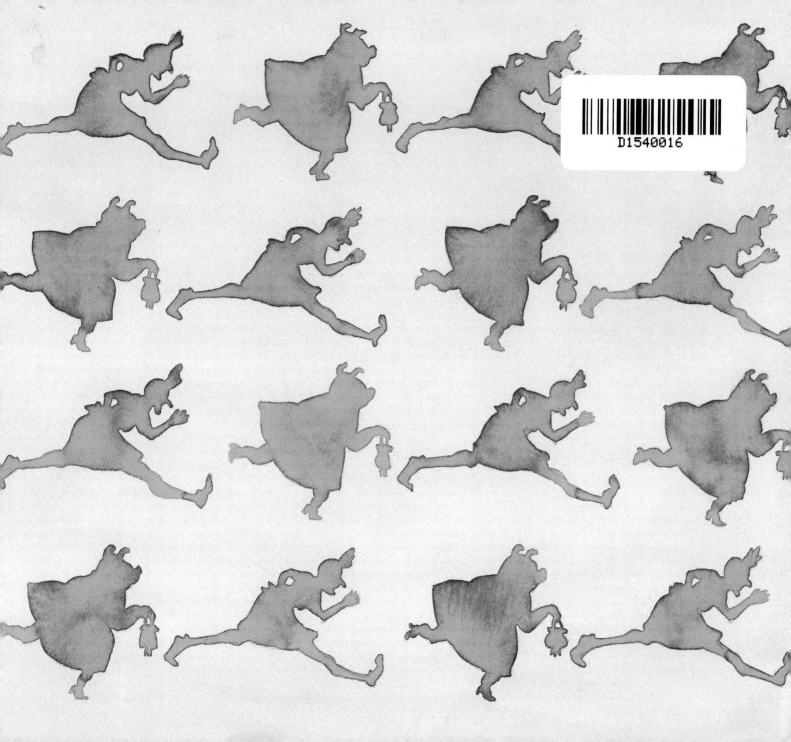

For my mother and father

1 2 3 4 5 6 7 8 9 10

Library of Congress Cataloging in Publication Data
Lewis, Bobby, (date)
  Home before midnight.
  For 2-6 year olds.
  Summary: In this cumulative nursery tale, an old woman needs a lot of
help to get her pig over the stile so she can get home before midnight.
  [1. Folklore] I. Title.
PZ8.1.L444Ho   398.2   [E]   81-6072
ISBN 0-688-00530-6   AACR2
ISBN 0-688-00731-7 (lib. bdg.)

HOME BEFORE MIDNIGHT

A TRADITIONAL VERSE
ILLUSTRATED BY BOBBY LEWIS

LOTHROP, LEE & SHEPARD BOOKS

Nellie Bones was sweeping her house and she found a crooked sixpence.

So she went to the market and bought a pig.

But as she was coming home she came to a stile,

and the piggy would not go over the stile. She went a little further and she met a dog.

So she said to him, "Dog! Dog! Bite pig. Piggy won't go over the stile; and I shan't get home till midnight."

But the dog wouldn't.

She went a little further and she met a stick.

So she said, "Stick! Stick! Beat dog. Dog won't bite pig; piggy won't go over the stile; and I shan't get home till midnight."

But the stick wouldn't.

She went a little further and she met a fire.

So she said, "Fire! Fire! Burn stick. Stick won't beat dog; dog won't bite pig; piggy won't go over the stile; and I shan't get home till midnight."

But the fire wouldn't.

So she went a little further and she met some water.

So she said, "Water! Water! Quench fire. Fire won't burn stick; stick won't beat dog; dog won't bite pig; piggy won't go over the stile; and I shan't get home till midnight."

But the water wouldn't.

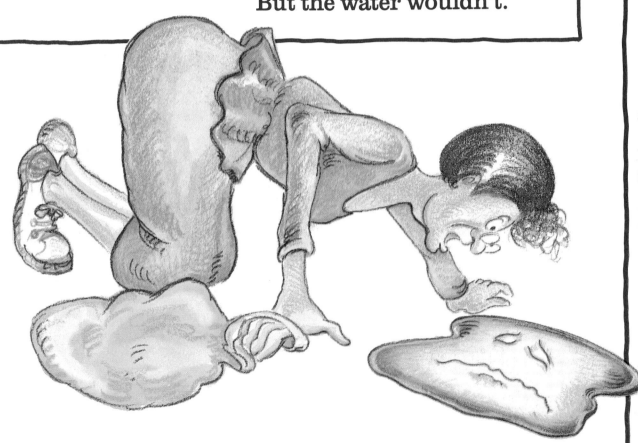

She went a little further and she met an ox.

So she said, "Ox! Ox! Drink water. Water won't quench fire; fire won't burn stick; stick won't beat dog; dog won't bite pig; piggy won't go over the stile; and I shan't get home till midnight."

But the ox wouldn't.

She went a little further and she met a butcher. So she said, "Butcher! Butcher! Kill ox.

"Ox won't drink water; water won't quench fire; fire won't burn stick; stick won't beat dog; dog won't bite pig; piggy won't go over the stile; and I shan't get home till midnight."

But the butcher wouldn't.

She went a little further and she met a rope. So she said, "Rope! Rope! Hang butcher. Butcher won't kill ox; ox won't drink water; water won't quench fire; fire won't burn stick; stick won't beat dog; dog won't bite pig; piggy won't go over the stile; and I shan't get home till midnight."

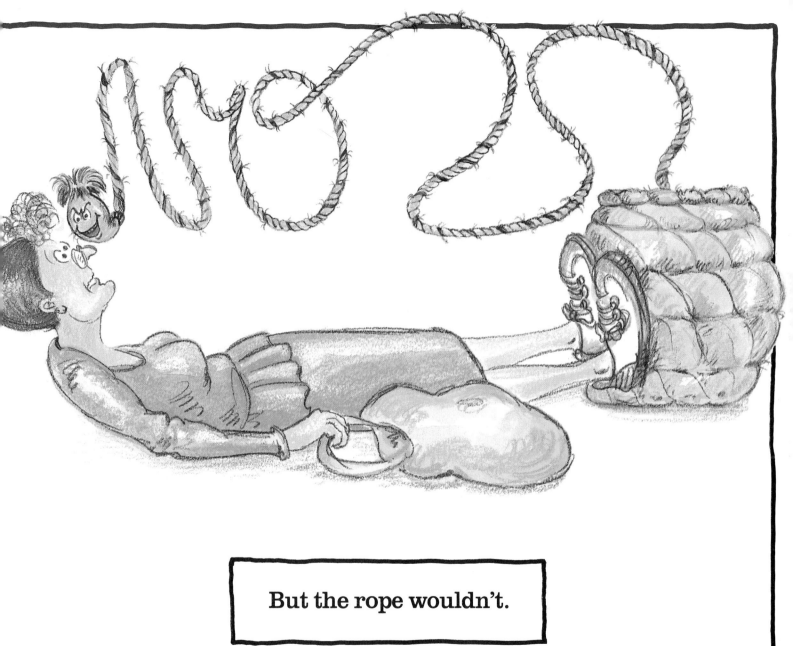

But the rope wouldn't.

So she went a little
further and she met a rat.
So she said, "Rat! Rat! Gnaw rope. Rope won't
hang butcher; butcher won't kill ox; ox won't
drink water; water won't quench fire; fire
won't burn stick; stick won't beat dog; dog
won't bite pig; piggy won't go over the stile;
and I shan't get home till midnight."

But the rat wouldn't.

She went a little further and she met a cat.

So she said, "Cat! Cat! Kill rat. Rat won't gnaw rope; rope won't hang butcher; butcher won't kill ox; ox won't drink water; water won't quench fire; fire won't burn stick; stick won't beat dog; dog won't bite pig; piggy won't go over the stile; and I shan't get home till midnight."

And the cat said to her, "If you will fetch me some milk, I will kill rat."

As soon as the cat had lapped up the milk, the cat began to kill the rat.

The rat began to gnaw the rope.

The rope began to hang the butcher. The butcher began to kill the ox.

The ox began to drink the water.

The water began to quench the fire.

The fire began to burn the stick.

The stick began to beat the dog. The dog began to bite the pig.

The pig jumped over the stile.

And so Nellie Bones got home before midnight.

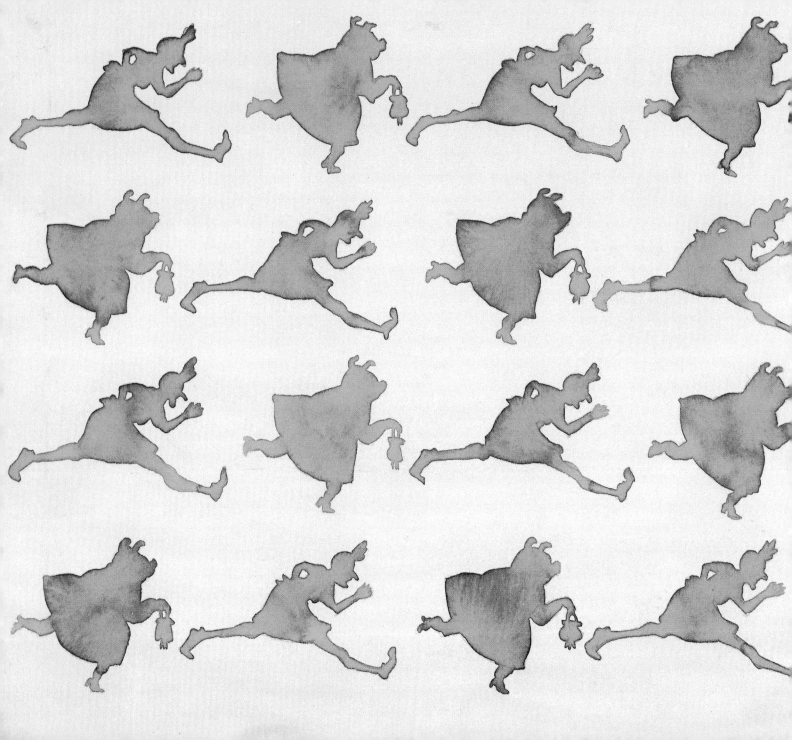